Mariana
the Goldilocks
Fairy

To baby bears everywhere, from the fairies

Special thanks to Rachel Elliot

ISBN 978-1-338-05499-6

10 9 8 7 6 5 4 3 2 1   17 18 19 20 21

Printed in the U.S.A.   40
First edition, March 2017

Mariana
the Goldilocks
Fairy
by Daisy Meadows

SCHOLASTIC INC.

The Fairyland Palace

Fairyland Library

The Three Bears' Cottage

Island

Thumbelina's Cottage

Storybook World

Rapunzel's Tower

Red Riding Hood's Grandmother's House

Red Riding Hood Woods

Jack Frost's Ice Castle

Storytelling Festival Site

Wetherbury Village

Story Barge

Riverbank

The fairies want stories to stay just the same.
But I've planned a funny and mischievous game.
I'll change all their tales without further ado,
By adding some tricks and a goblin or two!

The four magic stories will soon be improved
When everything that's nice and sweet is removed.
Their dull happy endings are ruined and lost,
For no one's as smart as handsome Jack Frost!

Contents

Puppet Problems

Kirsty Tate was walking along the river path toward the Story Barge, feeling thrilled to her fingertips. She loved books, and the Wetherbury Storytelling Festival was like a dream come true for her. Even better, she was enjoying every moment with her best friend, Rachel Walker, who was staying for the whole weekend.

"This day just gets better and better," said Rachel, grabbing Kirsty's hand. "The Storybook Picnic was amazing, and now we're going to see a puppet show put on by Alana Yarn. I can't wait!"

Alana Yarn was one of their favorite authors. She was running the festival, which was being held in Wetherbury Park. The girls were attending every event they could. They had just come from a giant picnic, where they had eaten food inspired by their favorite stories. There had even been a cake in the shape of a very large storybook.

"What was your favorite food at the picnic?" Kirsty asked as they reached the Story Barge.

"I can't decide," said Rachel after a

moment's pause. "I loved the *Alice in Wonderland* EAT ME cupcakes, but the *Peter Pan* cake pops were delicious, too."

They were standing next to the Story Barge now, and there was a sign on the path advertising the show.

ALANA YARN'S PUPPET SHOW

COME INSIDE AND GUESS THE STORY

"Come on!" said Kirsty.

She stepped onto the creaky old Story Barge. A short ladder led to the upper deck, which was piled with books. Inviting armchairs and plump floor cushions were scattered around. Lots of children were already on board, looking very excited.

"Let's find a seat," said Rachel. "I want to look at all these books."

The girls settled down on a large blue cushion, and they were soon sharing a book that they had been longing to read. Just as they finished the first chapter and exchanged happy smiles, a head popped up from the wooden staircase that led down to the lower deck of the barge. It was Alana Yarn.

"The puppet show is ready," she announced. "Come on down to the lower deck, everyone. A story is waiting for you!"

The children made their way
downstairs and gathered on large pillows
in the middle of the lower deck. At the
far end of the deck, Rachel and Kirsty
saw a small stage with a tall striped
puppet theater and a large trunk. The
trunk had a curved lid, decorated with
pictures of fairy tale characters. Alana
was standing in front of the trunk, and

as soon as all the children were sitting down, she lifted the lid.

"I'd like you to try to guess what story I'm going to tell," she told the listening children. "Look carefully at the puppets and see if you can figure it out."

First, she took out a large hand puppet of a girl with long blond hair. Then she placed some props on the stage.

Rachel and Kirsty watched as she set out three beds—one big, one small, and one medium-size. Next, three chairs appeared—one big, one small, and one medium-size. Finally, Alana took out three bowls of porridge and looked around with a smile.

"Any ideas?" she asked.

Almost all the children raised their hands, looking excited. Alana nodded at Rachel.

"I think the puppet show is going to be about Goldilocks," she said.

"That's right," said Alana with a laugh. "Now, I wonder if the girl next to you can guess which puppets I will bring out of the trunk next?"

Kirsty laughed, too.

"Of course," she said. "The three bears."

A puzzled look crossed Alana's face.

"No, that's not right," she said, sounding confused.

Rachel and Kirsty glanced at each other in surprise. If they weren't the three bears, what could the puppets be?

Alana reached into the trunk and pulled out three green puppets— complete with big feet, bumpy heads, and long noses.

They were goblins!

Into the Book World

The other children laughed as if Kirsty should have known.

"How could you think it was bears?" asked a boy sitting nearby. "Your friend just said that the story was Goldilocks."

"Yes, *Goldilocks and the Three Bears*," Kirsty agreed.

"Don't be silly," said the boy. "Everyone knows that it's Goldilocks and the Three Goblins."

The other children nodded in agreement.

"It's my favorite story," the boy went on. "I love how the three naughty goblins make such a mess in the cottage."

"That's not what happens," said Kirsty.

But no one except Rachel was listening. The girls shot each other an anxious look. They knew exactly what was going on.

That morning, Rachel and

Kirsty had met Elle the Thumbelina Fairy. She had whisked them to Fairyland, where they had met the rest of the Storybook Fairies—Mariana the Goldilocks Fairy, Rosalie the Rapunzel Fairy, and Ruth the Red Riding Hood Fairy. They were all very upset. Jack Frost and his goblins had stolen their magical objects, and their stories were in danger of being ruined forever.

Whoever held the magical objects had control of the stories. The fairies always used their objects to make sure the stories went how they were supposed to and ended well. But Jack Frost and the goblins wanted the stories to be all about them, so they were using the magical objects to go into the stories and change them.

The girls had already followed the goblins into the story of Thumbelina, and helped her marry her flower prince. But there were still three more magical objects to find.

"I'm so happy that we were able to help Elle get her magic thumb ring back from the goblins this morning," Kirsty whispered. "But it looks as if Mariana the Goldilocks Fairy will need our help, too. Someone is inside the story right now, changing the bears into goblins!"

"Before the story starts, would anyone like to come up to the stage and look at the puppets and props?" Alana asked.

The children sprang to their feet and hurried over to the puppet theater. Everyone wanted to have a closer look at the beautiful puppets. But Rachel and

Kirsty held back and stood next to the props table. They looked at each other worriedly.

"What should we do?" asked Rachel. "It's obvious that there are goblins inside the story of Goldilocks right now. How can we stop them?"

Kirsty bit her lip. "The fairy dust in our lockets would take us to Fairyland, but we wouldn't know where to find the Storybook Fairies. Besides, we need to get into the story of Goldilocks, and I don't think our fairy dust can do that."

She rested her hand on the table and accidentally knocked over one of the porridge bowls with a clatter. She picked it up, and Mariana the Goldilocks Fairy fluttered out from underneath it! She was wearing a blue dress, and her red shoes perfectly matched the bow in her golden hair.

"Hooray, I found you!" Mariana exclaimed. "I wasn't sure if I'd be able to get you away from the other children. Come quickly. We need to find a place to hide so we can talk."

"This way," said Rachel, darting behind the puppet theater.

Kirsty followed her, with Mariana fluttering at her side. The other children were still crowding around the puppets, so no one noticed the girls slipping out of sight. When they were safely hidden behind the puppet theater, the girls looked up at Mariana with eager smiles.

"We're so glad you're here," said Kirsty. "Something has happened to the Goldilocks story, and we think that the goblins must be inside it right now."

"They are," Mariana said. "That's

why I'm here.
They have
my magic
spoon,
which
means
that
they can
change
whatever
they want
in the story.

It's a disaster! I have to find a way to make the Goldilocks story go the way it's supposed to."

"Yes, it should have three bears, not three goblins," said Rachel.

"Exactly," Mariana agreed. "Elle told me how amazing you were this morning, helping her get her magical thumb ring back from the goblins. Do you think you might be able to help me, too?"

"Of course we can," said Kirsty at once. "We can't allow Jack Frost and his goblins to ruin the best stories in the world."

A smile spread across Mariana's face, and she pulled a tiny book from her pocket. She held it out to the girls, and they leaned closer. The title was

written in tiny golden letters: *Goldilocks*.
Mariana opened the book. The writing
was so small that Rachel and Kirsty
couldn't read it. But Mariana tapped
the page with her wand, and a twist of
golden sparkles spun out of the book.
The twist grew bigger, until it swept the
girls up, and all they could see was the
glimmer of gold. They heard Mariana's
voice above the whoosh of the swirling
fairy dust.

"The Goldilocks story needs magical repairs.

We must stop the goblins and find the three bears.

Together I know we can quickly succeed,

And the goblins will feel very foolish indeed!"

Book World Bears

Gasping, the girls landed in a pile of leaves. They looked around and saw that they were just outside the white fence of a little cottage in the woods. They could hear birds twittering in the tree branches, and fluffy white clouds floated overhead.

"It all seems very peaceful," said Rachel, feeling puzzled. "I thought that the goblins would be here already, causing mischief."

Suddenly, the door of the cottage banged open, and a little girl with blond ringlets burst out. She ran down the garden path and slammed the gate behind her.

"Are you all right?" Kirsty asked the girl, as she and Rachel scrambled to their feet.

"I hope you're not going into the cottage," said the girl, panting. "It's a total mess! I couldn't wait to get out of there—it's horrible!"

"Wait, are you Goldilocks?" asked
Rachel. "Aren't you supposed to be inside
the cottage, trying out the different chairs
and the beds?"

"I'm not going to sit on any chairs or
lie on any beds in there," said Goldilocks.
"It's filthy!"

She tossed her ringlets and ran off into
the woods. Rachel and Kirsty exchanged
worried glances.

"Come on," said Mariana. "We have to find out what's going on in there."

She fluttered over the gate, and the girls hurried up the path. Goldilocks had left the door swinging open on its hinges, and Rachel gave a loud knock and waited. No one came to the door.

"Oh no—Goldilocks was right," said Kirsty, peering in through the doorway. "It's a terrible mess in here."

They stepped into the cottage. The front door led straight into the kitchen, which was a wreck. Every single pot, pan, and plate seemed to be on the floor. Pieces of broken china were scattered around, and almost all the cabinet doors were open. Someone had burst a bag of flour, coating everything in white powder. Tomato sauce was all over the table and it looked like someone had made splotches on the wall. The kitchen faucet was running, and the sink was about to overflow. Rachel darted over and turned the water off.

"This is awful," said Mariana. "The three bears usually keep this cottage spic-and-span. I can't believe that they would leave it in this state."

"I'm sure they didn't," said Rachel, pointing to the floor. "Look—I think the goblins have been here."

There were large, muddy footprints all over the kitchen tiles.

"Those are definitely goblin prints," said Kirsty. "But they're not here now."

Rachel stepped back outside the cottage, looking down at the path.

"There are more prints here," she said.

"Let's follow them," said Kirsty. "If we can find the goblins, we might be able to get Mariana's magic spoon back."

"Wait—these aren't goblin footprints,"

said Rachel, kneeling down. "These are paw prints—big ones, medium-size ones, and little ones."

"The three bears!" cried Mariana. "It must be them. We have to follow them and find out what happened here."

Rachel stood up and followed the prints down the path.

"It looks like they went into the forest," she said. "It might take us a long time to track them down—bears will be able to move through the forest more quickly than us."

"Not if you can fly like me," said Mariana with a smile.

She waved her wand, and the air shimmered with magic as Rachel and Kirsty shrank to fairy size. Seconds later they were fluttering beside Mariana with gauzy wings.

"Let's go!"
said Kirsty.
"We have
to find
the bears
and find
out what the
goblins have
been doing."
The paw
prints led the
fairies toward the middle of the forest.
It grew darker as they went deeper, and
they were surrounded by strange noises.
Kirsty reached out her hand, and Rachel
squeezed it.

"I'm glad you're here," Kirsty
whispered. "This forest is a little spooky!"

Rachel smiled at her. Suddenly, Mariana

let out a squeak of
excitement.

"I see
them!" she
exclaimed.
"Look!"

The
fairies
were flying
toward
a huge
thick oak
tree, which
looked strong and
ancient. Its branches
reached up so high that they couldn't
see the top. On the branch closest to the
ground, a baby bear was snuffling his
little nose. A medium-size mother bear

was sitting on the
branch above, and
a few branches
farther up
was a very
big father bear.
The baby bear
was trembling so
much that
the leaves
on the
tree were
shaking.

"What's wrong?" asked Mariana, rushing to the biggest bear.

"Don't be upset!" cried Kirsty, fluttering over to the mother bear.

"There's nothing to be afraid of," said Rachel, hovering beside the baby bear. "We're here to help. What happened?"

Just Right!

"It's been so scary," said Mama Bear, her voice shaking. "But the day started happily. We were playing in the woods, and it was so sunny out that we decided to go home and pack a picnic for lunch."

"But when we got home, we heard a terrible racket inside our cottage," Papa Bear went on.

"I peeked through the windows," said Baby Bear, "and I saw three scary green creatures inside. They were horrible! They had big feet and long noses, and really mean expressions."

Kirsty and Rachel exchanged a knowing glance. The goblins!

"They were making a terrible mess," said Papa Bear. "We ran back into the woods to hide. We don't want any trouble. Why would they be so mean?"

"Because they're goblins," said Rachel with a sigh. "That's their idea of fun."

"I'm too scared to go back home," said Mama Bear. "But we didn't pack our picnic, and Baby Bear is very hungry.

We don't know what to do!"

"We've just been to your cottage," said Kirsty. "It was a mess, but the goblins were gone. It's safe for you to go home."

"Besides, we'll come with you," Mariana added.

"And we know the goblins," said Rachel. "We won't let them scare you again."

"I don't know," said Mama Bear.

But Baby Bear's tummy gave a big, hungry rumble, and he looked up at his parents.

"Please, let's go home," he said. "I want dinner!"

Soon, the three bears were hurrying through the woods, while the fairies fluttered beside them. But when they reached the cottage, they all stopped in dismay. There was a lot of noise coming from inside. They could hear bangs, crashes, and high-pitched squawks. The goblins were back.

"I've changed my mind," said Baby Bear, his voice shaking. "I'm not hungry after all."

"We'll just stay in the woods," Mama Bear added.

"We won't let the goblins drive you out of your home," said Kirsty. "Wait here and we will go talk to them."

The bears retreated behind the nearest tree, while the fairies flew over the fence.

"There's an open window here!" called Mariana.

They flew into the kitchen and landed on the drying rack. The three goblins had made even more of a mess than before, but now they were sitting around the table in front of three bowls of porridge. They were all wearing blue overalls and straw hats.

"Yum, yum!" said the smallest goblin. "Porridge is the best!"

"Especially when it belongs to someone else," added the medium-size goblin with a snicker.

They each took a spoonful of their porridge.

"Ow!" shrieked the smallest goblin. "Too ho-ho-hot!"

"Yuck!" grumbled the biggest goblin.

"It's stone cold!"

But the medium-size goblin said nothing at all. He was too busy gobbling down his porridge. Mariana took a step forward.

"Look!" she said suddenly. "The medium-size goblin is using my magic spoon to eat his porridge!"

He ate and ate with it until his bowl was scraped clean. Then he leaned back and patted his tummy.

"Just right," he said in a smug voice.

"Maybe he will forget to pick the spoon up," Kirsty whispered. "One of us could grab it."

But just then, the goblin reached out a bony hand, picked up the spoon, and licked it clean. Then he tucked it into the back pocket of his overalls.

Disappointed, the fairies slipped out of sight behind a saucepan and kept watching. The smallest goblin got up and walked over to the fireplace, where three chairs were gathered around the fire. He sat down in the smallest chair. The medium-size goblin plonked himself down in the medium-size chair, and the biggest goblin took the biggest chair.

"This chair is too little for me," the smallest goblin grumbled. "My bottom keeps getting stuck, and it's too hard and uncomfortable."

"Well this one is too big and squishy for me," the biggest goblin complained. "It's swallowing me up!"

Only the medium-size goblin looked happy.

"This one is just right," he said. "I'm so

smart—I picked the best one."

"Oh, is that so?" huffed the biggest goblin. "We'll see about that!"

He tipped the medium-size goblin out of the medium-size chair and sat down in it himself. Squawking with fury, the other two goblins started to push and prod him, trying to get him to move.

"I should have the 'just right' chair!" wailed the smallest goblin. "I'm the little one!"

The medium-size goblin sat on the lap of the biggest goblin and bounced up and down. They fell to the floor together, shouting and scratching at each other.

"This is our chance!" Rachel whispered.

Food Fight

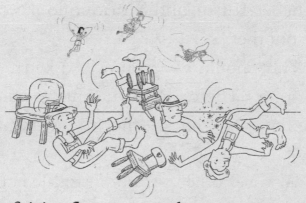

The fairies flew across the room to try to take the spoon while the goblins were squabbling, but the goblins were rolling around on the floor too quickly. Then the smallest goblin clambered onto the "just right" chair, and the others let out shouts of fury. The biggest goblin shoved him, and he fell to the floor with a loud thump.

"You're so mean to me!" he wailed. "I'm not playing with you anymore!"

He scrambled away and raced upstairs, closely followed by the other two goblins.

Rachel, Kirsty, and Mariana looked at one another.

"What should we do now?" asked Mariana. "There's no way that we can take the spoon back—they're moving too fast."

"We have to keep trying," said Kirsty in a determined voice. "Come on!"

They zoomed up the stairs and into the bedroom, which had three beds in it. Fluttering against the ceiling, they watched the goblins jump up and down on the biggest bed.

"Awful!" shouted the smallest goblin. "This one's got no bounce at all—it's much too soft!"

They all leaped onto the next bed, which was medium-size. As they jumped, the bed made a cracking sound.

"They're going to break it!" Rachel exclaimed.

"They don't care," said Mariana.

"Hopeless!" the biggest goblin squawked. "This bed is too hard. It's like trying to bounce on a piece of wood!"

They leapfrogged onto the last and smallest bed. Now they were so close together that their tummies were touching. But they had big smiles on their faces, and they all started to giggle.

"Wheeee!" squealed the medium-size goblin. "This is just right!"

"Now's our chance," said Rachel as the goblins jumped higher and higher. "We have to fly up behind the goblin with the spoon and take it out of his pocket before he spots us."

"It's very risky," said Mariana, turning pale.

Rachel and Kirsty took her hands.

"Be brave, Mariana," said Kirsty. "We

can do it!"

The fairies flew across the ceiling to the curtains and then fluttered down behind them, keeping out of sight.

"Let's get under the bed and then fly up together," said Rachel. "Hopefully one of us will be able to take the spoon."

They swooped down and flew under the biggest bed and the medium-size bed toward the goblins. When they were under the smallest bed, Rachel held up three fingers and counted down, to make sure that they would all fly out at exactly the same moment. Three . . . two . . . one . . .

Whoosh! They zipped upward, but just at that moment the smallest goblin jumped off the bed and spotted them.

"Fairies!" he yelled. "This place is infested with fairies! Run!"

All three goblins bounced off the bed and scurried downstairs to the kitchen. Rachel, Kirsty, and Mariana followed them past the fireside chairs and toward the kitchen table. The porridge bowls were still there, and two of them had hardly been touched. The goblins dove under the table.

"I've got an idea!" said Kirsty with a gasp. "Mariana, can you make us human-size again? I think I know a way to make him take the spoon out of his pocket."

Mariana swished her wand through the air, and instantly Rachel and Kirsty were girls again. Kirsty darted over to the table and picked up one of the spoons. Then she peered under the table.

"Come out from under there!" she demanded.

The goblins scrambled out, staring at her in astonishment.

"How did you get there?" asked the biggest goblin.

"Where are the fairies?" asked the medium-size goblin.

Kirsty didn't reply. She just scooped up a big spoonful of porridge, took a deep breath, and catapulted it at the medium-size goblin. *Splat!* It hit him square on the forehead.

"Porridge fight!" he squealed, sounding delighted.

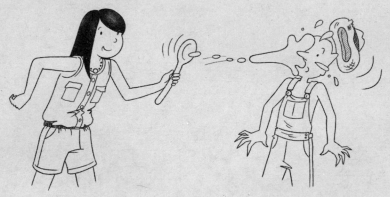

He pulled the magic spoon out of his back pocket, dug it into the other bowl of porridge, and flung a cold lump of it at Kirsty. The other goblins grabbed spoons and started to fling porridge around, too. Soon they had forgotten about the girls and were hurling cold porridge at one another. Kirsty and Rachel ducked behind an armchair as porridge flew over their heads and goblin shrieks filled the air. Mariana was hiding behind a curtain.

"At least the magic spoon is out of the goblin's pocket," said Rachel. "Now we have to get it back for Mariana!"

A lump of porridge hit the wall nearby and Kirsty winced.

"I know it was bad to start a food fight," she said. "I just couldn't think of any other way to get the spoon back."

"You did the right thing," said Rachel. "We can clean up afterward. Besides, I've got a plan . . ."

Three Goblins, Three Bears, and a Picnic

The girls peeked out from behind the chair. There was porridge all over the kitchen. The walls were dripping, and the counters and floor were covered in slippery porridge puddles. Rachel took Kirsty's spoon, stood up, and launched another blob of porridge at the medium-size goblin. Then she backed away toward the stairs, followed by Kirsty.

"Come back here!" the goblin barked.

He tried to run after them, but skidded on a porridge puddle and skated across the floor with his arms flapping. The magic spoon flew out of his hand.

"No!" shouted the other goblins.

They dove toward the magic spoon, belly flopping onto the porridge, and went sliding across the floor on their tummies.

The magic spoon landed in Kirsty's hand, and the goblins groaned as her fingers closed around it. Flapping around in the porridge, they watched as Kirsty held out the spoon to Mariana. The little fairy fluttered out of her hiding place and took the spoon. It immediately shrank to fairy size, and glowed for a moment as if it were glad to be back in her hand. Mariana's eyes shone with happiness.

"Hooray!" cried Rachel, clapping her hands.

"It's not fair!" wailed the smallest goblin.

Just then, there was a noise at the door. The girls looked up and saw the three bears peeking in. They all looked nervous, but when they saw the goblins, their expressions changed. Their eyes crinkled at the corners, their mouths twitched, and then they started to laugh.

"Hee, hee," said Mama Bear with her paw over her mouth. "Now that they're covered in porridge, they don't look scary anymore."

"They just look silly!" added Baby Bear.

The goblins looked around. When they
saw the big bears looming over them,
they all squealed.

"Help!" shouted the biggest goblin.

"We're all going
to be eaten!"
wailed the
medium-
size
goblin.

"Run!"
the smallest
goblin
shrieked.

The goblins dove out the kitchen
window, and the bears stepped into their
home.

"Oh dear, look at this mess," said
Mama Bear with a groan.

"Don't worry," said Mariana, fluttering forward.

She waved her wand, and the porridge disappeared from the walls, floors, table, and counters. The pots and pans danced their way back into the cabinets, and soon everything was tidy and sparkling clean. In a final flurry of sparkles, a picnic basket appeared on the kitchen table.

"Honey sandwiches," said Mariana with a smile. "You must all be very hungry by now."

"Thank you!" said the bears in delight.

They picked up the picnic basket and set off into the forest again, waving good-bye as they went. Mariana turned to the girls.

"How can I ever thank you?" she asked.

"There's no need," Rachel replied.

"Oh, yes there is," said Mariana. "And

I know just the way! My porridge is famous, and I am going to make a pot for you—right now."

With a whispered spell and a wave of her wand, a pot of porridge appeared on the kitchen table. The aroma was mouth-watering, and the girls could hardly wait to try it.

"Delicious!" said Kirsty when she took her first mouthful. "Not too hot and not too cold."

"Not too salty and not too sweet," Rachel added. "It's just right!"

When they had finished eating, Mariana raised her wand.

"Time to go back to the human world," she said. "I will never forget your bravery and kindness today. Thank you!"

As Mariana's wand swished and the girls waved, they glimpsed someone through the kitchen window. It was Goldilocks, and she was walking up the path toward the cottage.

"Everything is turning out as it should," said Kirsty, as the cottage melted away around them.

Suddenly they were back on the Story Barge, behind the striped puppet theater. Not a moment had passed since they had set off on their magical adventure. They went back to join the other children as Alana Yarn clapped her hands together.

"All right, everyone, this puppet show needs volunteers!" she said. "Who would like to help me tell this story?"

The other children hesitated, but Rachel stepped forward. Alana smiled at her.

"Thank you for being the first volunteer," she said. "I'd like you to operate the Goldilocks puppet."

Smiling from ear to ear, Rachel picked up her puppet.

"Now, I need volunteers to work the puppets for the three"—Rachel and Kirsty held their breath—"bears!"

Kirsty's hand shot into the air, and she was picked along with two other children.

"You can be Baby Bear," Alana told Kirsty. "Now, everyone else, take your seats. The show is about to begin!"

The puppet show went perfectly. At the end, when the three bears returned from their picnic to find Goldilocks in their cottage, Kirsty caught Rachel's eye and they exchanged a smile of relief. The story of *Goldilocks and the Three Bears* had been saved, and they couldn't wait to save the rest of the Storybook Fairies' stories!

RAINBOW magic

THE STORYBOOK FAIRIES

Rachel and Kirsty found Elle's
and Mariana's missing magic
objects. Now it's time for
them to help

Rosalie
the Rapunzel Fairy!

Join their next adventure in
this special sneak peek …

Intruder in the Tower

"Hurry up, Kirsty," called Rachel Walker, skipping past colorful bunting and festival tents. "I can't wait to get to the Story Barge."

Her best friend, Kirsty Tate, had paused to look at a tent that was decorated with the first lines of lots of different children's books. She grinned at Rachel and ran to catch up to her.

"That tent is amazing," she said. "I want to make sure I go back later and see how many first lines I recognize."

Rachel and Kirsty were having a wonderful weekend. Rachel was staying with Kirsty so that they could go to the Wetherbury Storytelling Festival together. One of their favorite authors, Alana Yarn, was leading the festival and had arranged lots of fun storytelling activities.

"We did so much yesterday, it feels like we've had a whole weekend already," said Rachel. "There was the *Goldilocks* puppet show and Alana's storytelling performance of *Thumbelina*."

"And we met the Storybook Fairies," Kirsty added, remembering the magical adventures they had shared with Elle the Thumbelina Fairy and Mariana the Goldilocks Fairy.

"And we still have all of Sunday ahead of us," said Rachel, stopping to do a cartwheel. "I'm so excited! I wonder what Alana has planned for today."

"I hope we see the Storybook Fairies again," Kirsty added.

"I'm sure we will," said Rachel. "After all, there are still two magical objects to find."

The girls were secret friends of Fairyland, but this was the first time that they had met the Storybook Fairies. Elle the Thumbelina Fairy had asked Rachel and Kirsty to help them because Jack Frost had stolen their magical objects. Rachel and Kirsty had already helped

Elle and Mariana get their magical objects back, but Rosalie the Rapunzel Fairy and Ruth the Red Riding Hood Fairy were still missing theirs.

The river was sparkling in the sunshine, and as they got closer to the Story Barge, the girls saw Alana Yarn standing on the path. When she saw them, she gave a mysterious smile.

"This morning's activity is in a very special place," she said. "Go to the playground by the river and look for a tower. Then see if you can figure out what this morning's story is all about!"

Kirsty and Rachel exchanged excited smiles. They waved to Alana and raced off along the path to the playground.

"This is the best playground in Wetherbury," Kirsty told Rachel.

It was the biggest playground that Rachel had ever seen. There were lots of colorful swings, a merry-go-round, and seesaws, all surrounded by a bright yellow fence. There were horses on springs, jungle gyms, tunnels, and even a speaking tube. In the center of the playground was a big slide, with a tall winding ladder that led to a tower at the top.

RAINBOW magic™

Which Magical Fairies Have You Met?

- ❑ The Rainbow Fairies
- ❑ The Weather Fairies
- ❑ The Jewel Fairies
- ❑ The Pet Fairies
- ❑ The Sports Fairies
- ❑ The Ocean Fairies
- ❑ The Princess Fairies
- ❑ The Superstar Fairies
- ❑ The Fashion Fairies
- ❑ The Sugar & Spice Fairies
- ❑ The Earth Fairies
- ❑ The Magical Crafts Fairies
- ❑ The Baby Animal Rescue Fairies
- ❑ The Fairy Tale Fairies
- ❑ The School Day Fairies

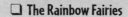

Find all of your favorite fairy friends at
scholastic.com/rainbowmagic

HIT entertainment

RMFAIRY